This book belongs to:

_____

Rex

Prakash

MAYA

Kit

Sam & Tom

SOPHIE

George

BABY YOGA @ 2pm

EMILY

HONEY

Winnie

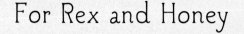

For Rex and Honey

Yoga is such a wonderful activity for all the family and has a hugely calming impact all round. It's great for coordination as well as health and wellbeing. It's also lots of fun! I love doing yoga with my kids but I'm not a yoga teacher. The text and illustrations in this book have been approved by a qualified yoga instructor, but *Yoga Babies* was not written as a 'How-to' guide. Baby yoga is something fun for you to do **with** your kids – so please don't leave them unsupervised while they're trying poses. Hope you enjoy reading this together and meeting my gorgeous Yoga Babies.

Fearne X

This paperback edition first published in 2018 by Andersen Press Ltd.
First published in Great Britain in 2017 by Andersen Press Ltd.,
20 Vauxhall Bridge Road, London SW1V 2SA.

Text copyright © Fearne Cotton 2017. Illustration copyright © Sheena Dempsey 2017.
The rights of Fearne Cotton and Sheena Dempsey to be identified as the author and
illustrator of this work have been asserted by them in accordance with the
Copyright, Designs and Patents Act, 1988. All rights reserved.
Printed and bound in China. 10 9 8 7 6 5 4 3 2 1
British Library Cataloguing in Publication Data available.
ISBN 978 1 78344 659 9

FEARNE COTTON
Yoga Babies

Illustrated by SHEENA DEMPSEY

ANDERSEN PRESS

We're the Yoga Babies,
look what we can do.

George can sit up straight like this.
Can you do
it too?

This is little Honey,
she likes to touch her nose.

Not with her little fingers,
she does it with her toes!

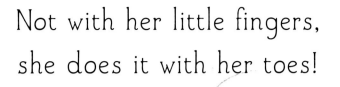

Maya's made a clever bridge,
see how she's arched her back.

Who's pushed his car right under her?
That's cheeky brother Jack!

We're the Yoga Babies,
look what we can do:
Rex can make the downward dog.
Can you do it too?

rex

Sophie and her mummy
have had a dreadful day

Ben was sick...

the car broke
down...

and then Tiggs ran away.

"Yoga time!" says Mummy.
"Now deep breath and relax."

But sometimes that is hard to do
with someone on your back!

Two mice on the carpet,
curled up so, so tight.
It's Tom and Sam in dormouse pose –
they'll sleep well tonight.

Prakash and his granny
are sitting on the floor,
playing SO BIG stretching games
while Prakash shouts out, "More!"

We're the Yoga Babies.
Look what we can do:
Winnie is a butterfly,
can you be one too?

Outside in the garden,
can you see a tree?
Tall and straight with not much wobble.
Well done, Emily!

Stretching in the sunshine,
Dad and Kit on mats,
curling downwards just like this –
till they look like cats.

Yes we're the Yoga Babies
from our toes up to our heads.

Stretching, breathing, having fun...

... then snuggling in our beds.

Cat Pose

RAINBOW POSE

Happy Baby Pose

Dormouse Pose

DOWNWARD DOG

Bear and Bunny Breathing

BRIDGE POSE

Child's Pose

TREE POSE

BUTTERFLY POSE